When Sophie Thinks She Can't...

by MOLLY BANG

with Ann Stern

THE BLUE SKY PRESS

An Imprint of Scholastic Inc. • New York

TO CHLOE, ELOISE, ISABELLE, SAGAN, IZZY,
CARTIER, JULIET, AND GRAY

Special thanks to Kathy Westray, who goes the extra hundred miles.

THE BLUE SKY PRESS

Library of Congress catalog card number available

ISBN 978-1-338-15298-2

10 9 8 7 6 5   20 21 22 23

Printed in China   38
First edition, January 2018

Book design by Molly Bang
and Kathleen Westray

Sophie loves working in the vegetable garden and exploring the woods.

But today, it's pouring rain, and Sophie's inside, trying and trying to build puzzle pieces into a square.

Sophie's sister walks by.

She moves the pieces,
and suddenly they
all fit perfectly.

"Too bad you're not smart," says her sister. And she walks away.

The next day is sunny. Not sunny for Sophie!

"I can't do ANYTHING!" she thinks.

She drags her feet all the way to school.

"How do we become smart?" asks Ms. Mulry.

Nobody knows the answer. They all think you have to be born smart.

"Flex those strong muscles of yours," says Ms. Mulry. All the children flex their muscles.

"Our muscles get stronger when we exercise, right? When we exercise our brains, by thinking hard, our brains get stronger, too!"

"Now, we've been learning about rectangles and squares."

RECTANGLE:

4 sides, 4 right angles,
opposite sides equal length
and parallel

SQUARE:

rectangle
with all sides
equal

"Today we'll exercise our brains with a math puzzle using squares and rectangles."

"But I can't do puzzles,"
Sophie thinks.

"I know I have
strong muscles.
I'm good at soccer,
and I work hard
in the garden."

"I CAN'T do PUZZLES,
and I'm NEVER smart at MATH."

But Ms. Mulry is talking.

"You're going to build a bigger rectangle out of twelve small squares.

How many different rectangles can you make?

Use the tools at your table, or come up with another way."

"I can't do it," says Sophie.

"Make your brain stronger," whispers Paula. "Just try."

Paula gathers up a pile of square tiles.

"Think hard, Sophie," whispers Andrew.
He takes a sheet of graph paper.
Sophie sits and stares.
And stares.

Maybe she can
draw them!

OH! Sophie does draw— squares. But her squares are all different sizes!

Paula has too many tiles!

Andrew's graph paper has too many little squares!

This problem is TOO HARD!!

Ms. Mulry is smiling.

She speaks to the class.

"*I see you mathematicians struggling.*"

You haven't
figured it
out . . .

YET.

Keep working!

Keep trying,
and you will."

Paula, Andrew, and Sophie work hard.
Paula takes only twelve tiles and
builds them into a rectangle.
Andrew marks a red X in each square
as he counts them.

Sophie thinks
of her garden.

Her garden is a
rectangle! The vegetables
are in straight lines!

Sophie draws a line with twelve different vegetables on it.

She draws squares around the twelve vegetables.

Paula, Andrew, and Sophie count
their different rectangles.
FOUR different kinds.

But Sophie is worried. "Mine's not
a rectangle," she groans. "It's too long!"

"It IS a rectangle," says Paula. "It's
a very LOOONNNNGGG one."

Meanwhile, Ms. Mulry looks at
the rectangles the other students
have made.

SIX Rectangles!
"You ALL did it!" she says.

SMARTER

"You've worked hard and gotten stuck. You've used the Most Important Word: YET.

You've tried and tried again,
helped each other—
and solved it!
Those brains of yours
have certainly gotten
stronger!"

Sophie feels the sun on her face. "I solved the puzzle!" She laughs. "And it was a MATH puzzle! I did it! I can do it again!"

"I'm getting SMARTER!"

When Sophie gets home, her dad has a puzzle, too.

"I can't figure out how to fix this cabinet door," he says.

"Dad," says Sophie, "you have to use the Most Important Word. You can't figure it out . . . YET. Can I help?"

And you know what?
They do fix it—together.

ABOUT THIS BOOK

Ann Stern has been a teacher of teachers for many years, and a good friend. We worked together long ago with middle-school students in Cambridge, Massachusetts.

Last year, Ann suggested that I write about "fixed" and "growth" mindsets, as the teachers she worked with were very excited by growth mindset teaching—and so was Ann!

Very simply, a person who has a fixed mindset believes intelligence is innate: It is fixed at birth, doesn't change, and determines what a person is capable of achieving. People with a fixed mindset believe a task is difficult because they aren't "smart," and they tend to give up.

But people with a growth mindset believe success can result from effort and effective strategies. When children are taught that we all have malleable intelligence and can "grow our brains" by forming new neural pathways, they become willing to struggle and persist with challenging tasks. When Ann taught teachers various ways to develop and nurture "growth" mindsets in their students, the teachers found their children were far more engaged in school-work and more persistent in responding to challenging work. They really enjoyed solving problems!

Ann and her husband, Ed, gave me the basic outline of this story and introduced me to the important research on mindsets by Carol Dweck and Jo Boaler. Most difficult was coming up with a math problem that was short, interesting, appropriate for young readers, and could be solved in several ways. Rachel Mulry—the real Ms. Mulry—came up with the problem in the book.

Ann and Ed also suggested I begin the story with Sophie trying to make the pieces of a tangram form the shape of a square. Tangrams—seven-piece geometric puzzles—were invented in China hundreds of years ago and are now used all over the world to teach math. At first, Sophie can't solve the puzzle. By the end of the story, we suspect she will keep trying—by seeing how her sister did it, rearranging the pieces, or . . . .

Can you make a tangram square? Can you make more figures from the pieces?